This book belongs to

Written by Jillian Harker
Illustrated by Gill McLean

This edition published by Parragon Books Ltd in 2015

Parragon Books Ltd
Chartist House
15–17 Trim Street
Bath BA1 1HA, UK
www.parragon.com

ISBN 978-1-4723-7723-4

Printed in China

Benji's New Friends

PaRRagon

Bath · New York · Cologne · Melbourne · Delhi
Hong Kong · Shenzhen · Singapore · Amsterdam

Benji sat on the end of the bed, feeling a little bit lonely. He was new here and he hadn't seen anyone else in the bedroom.

He watched a moonbeam slip through a gap in the curtains and slide across the bed.

"I wish that I had someone to play with," he whispered.

"Did I hear someone say they wanted to play?" asked a voice. The lid of the toy box flew open, and out climbed a dangly-legged, spotty horse.
"Hi, I'm Dottie… and I love to play!"

Boing!

Boing!

Dottie jumped onto the bed and began to
bounce up and down.

"Where did you come from?" she asked.

"From the birthday party," replied Benji.
"I was a present."

"Did someone mention a party?" A friendly-looking monkey poked his head around the curtain. "Why weren't Rosie and I invited?"

A floppy-eared rabbit appeared beside him.
"Max and I love parties!" Rosie the rabbit told
Benji. "And so does Humph."

She stared at the toy box. A loud yawn came
from inside. Then a bright-blue hippo slowly
lifted his head.

Party!

"A party!" said Humph. "That means food. And I'm hungry! Is there anything left to eat?"

"I think there are some cakes in the kitchen," replied Benji, "but do you think we should…?"

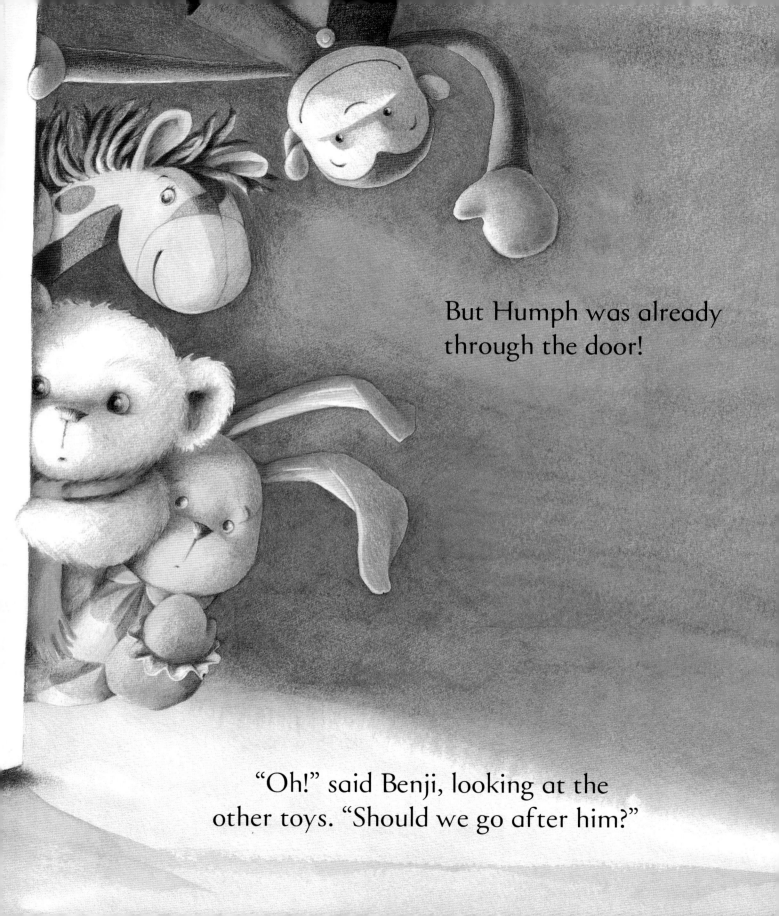

But Humph was already through the door!

"Oh!" said Benji, looking at the other toys. "Should we go after him?"

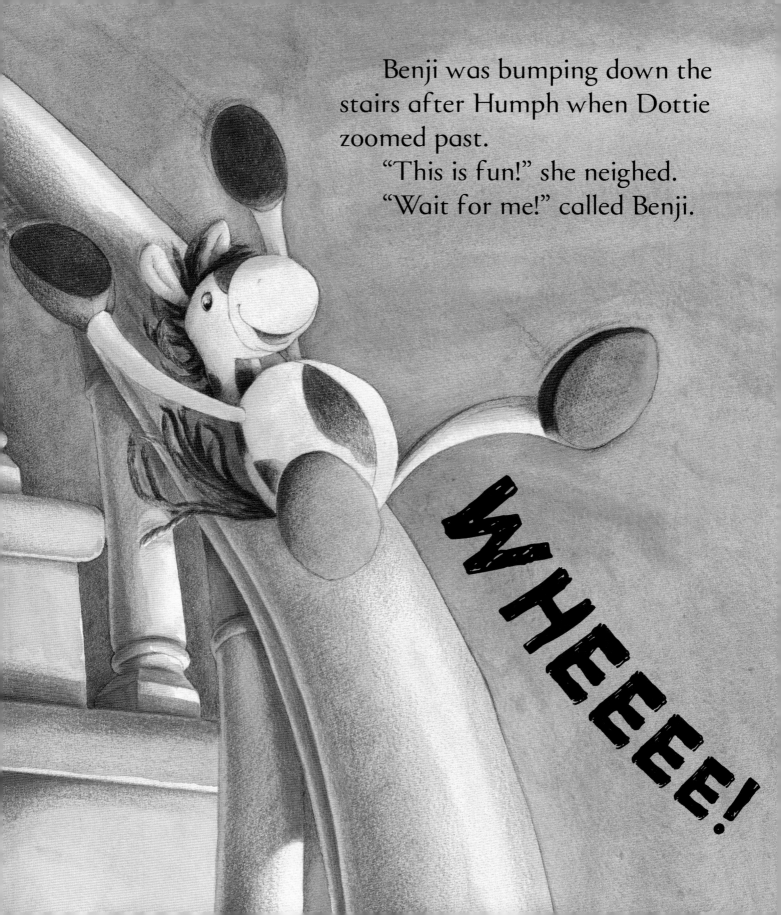

Benji was bumping down the stairs after Humph when Dottie zoomed past.

"This is fun!" she neighed.

"Wait for me!" called Benji.

WHEEEE!

In the kitchen, Humph was about to take
a bite out of a leftover cupcake. The candle
was already halfway into his mouth.

Before Benji could explain about the candle, he heard Dottie and Rosie yell loudly. They were staring at a large black shape outside the kitchen window.

They grabbed Benji and held on tight.

"It's just a cat," Benji said. "No need to worry."
"Phew," sighed Rosie with relief.
"I wish I could be as brave as you, Benji," laughed Dottie.

"That cat will stay outside, won't it?" whispered Max. They all looked to Benji for reassurance. Max had crept across the room and hidden under the table. Humph's knees were shaking.

There was a squeaking noise and then a loud **clatter!**

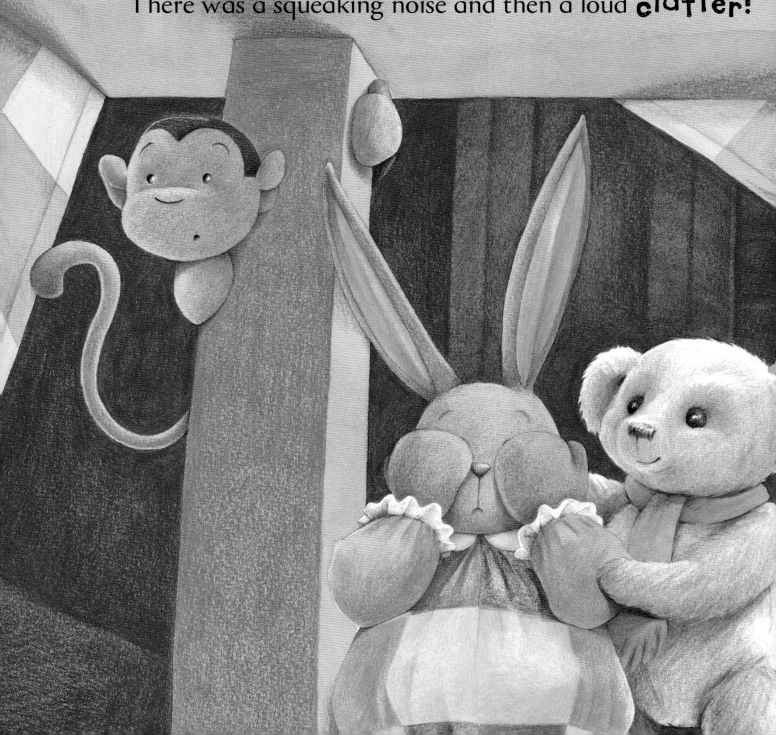

"Don't worry, that's just the cat coming into the kitchen," explained Benji. But Humph and Dottie, Max and Rosie had all raced out through the kitchen door and disappeared up the stairs as fast as their legs could carry them!

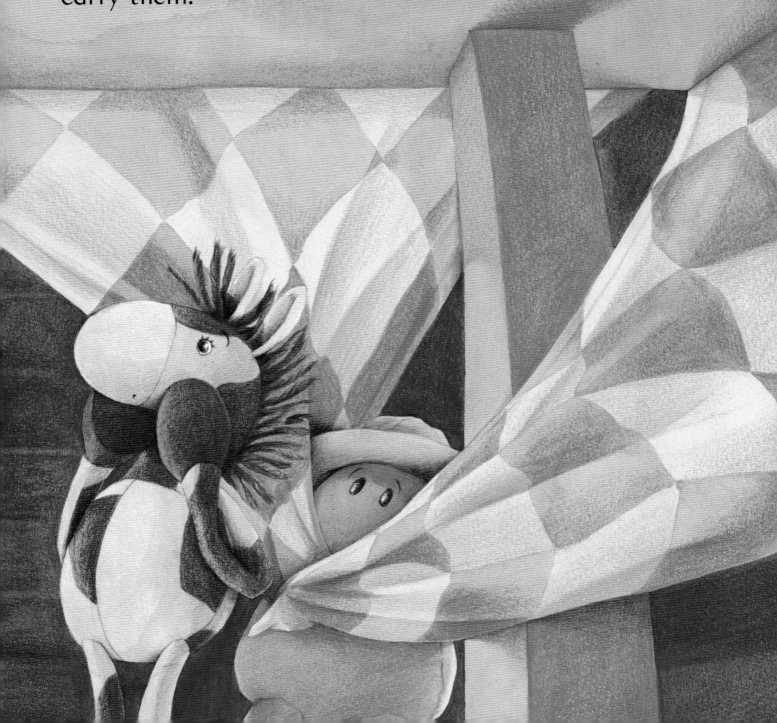

Benji found them all back in the bedroom. It took some time to persuade them to come out.

"Benji, will you always be here to look after us?" Dottie asked him.

Benji gave a tiny little smile. It was nice to feel wanted.

"Of course," he replied.

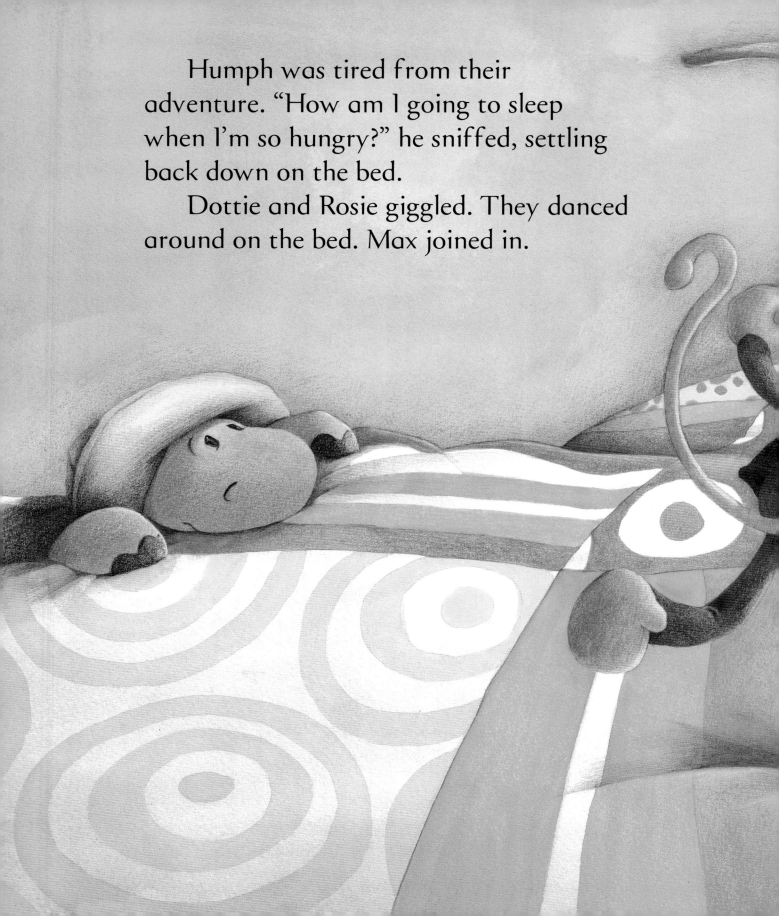

Humph was tired from their adventure. "How am I going to sleep when I'm so hungry?" he sniffed, settling back down on the bed.

Dottie and Rosie giggled. They danced around on the bed. Max joined in.

"Why don't we all play in the garden tomorrow?"
Rosie suggested.
"What's your garden like?" asked Benji.
"I'll show you," said Dottie, and she helped Benji
up to have a look out of the window.

"Wow!" he said. "It looks really exciting.
Are you going to play in the garden, Humph?"

"Humph!" said Humph sleepily. "It's such a long
way to the garden. I might just have a little nap
instead."

Benji smiled at his new sleepy friend.

Dottie jumped back onto the bed and started to bounce. Benji looked up at the moon. He had a feeling that he wouldn't be lonely any more.

"I wish that tomorrow will be as much fun as today," he whispered.

Then Benji turned to
his new friends and took
a huge leap, and began
to bounce on the bed.
"Here's to friends!"
he laughed.